To Hold this Ground

TO HOLD THIS GROUND

A DESPERATE BATTLE
AT GETTYSBURG

SUSAN PROVOST BELLER

illustrated with
twenty black-and-white photographs
and three maps

MARGARET K. MCELDERRY BOOKS

COPYRIGHT © 1995 BY SUSAN PROVOST BELLER
*All rights reserved including the right of
reproduction in whole or in part in any form.*
Margaret K. McElderry Books
An imprint of Simon & Schuster Children's Publishing Division
1230 Avenue of the Americas
New York, New York 10020

Designed by Carolyn Boschi

Maps prepared by Rick Britton

FIRST EDITION
Printed in the United States of America
1 3 5 7 9 10 8 6 4 2
The text of this book is set in Caslon 540.

Library of Congress Cataloging-in-Publication Data
Beller, Susan Provost
To hold this ground : a desperate battle at Gettysburg / Susan Provost Beller.
p.   cm.

*SUMMARY: A dramatic account of the battle for
Little Round Top at Gettysburg in 1863 as well as a biography of
Colonels Chamberlain of Maine and Oates of Alabama,
whose troops fought this bloody battle.
Includes bibliographical references and index.*
ISBN 0-689-50621-X
1. Gettysburg (Pa.), Battle of, 1863—Juvenile literature.   I. Title.
E475.53.B45   1995
973.7'349—dc20   94-12775

To my husband,
Walter Michael Beller,
who introduced me to Gettysburg,
his favorite battlefield,
so many years ago

ACKNOWLEDGMENTS

As always there are many people whose assistance in researching and preparing a book like this is priceless. My thanks to archivists of several collections, the Manuscript Reading Room at the Library of Congress, the United States Army Military History Institute, the Alabama Department of Archives and History, and the University of Vermont. Extensive assistance in selecting the right photographs came from Mary Ison, of the Library of Congress Prints and Photographs Division, Michael J. Winey, of the United States Army Military History Institute, and the staffs of the National Archives, the National Library of Medicine, the Alabama Archives, and the University of Vermont. Technical assistance with contemporary photographs was provided by Jim Weekes of Middlebury, Vermont.

I owe the greatest debt to my husband, Michael, whose extensive knowledge of this battle and the material written about it saved me countless hours of searching for the right quote or story. He also provided his always-excellent contemporary photographs and his thorough and insightful comments on the various drafts of the manuscript.

Thanks also to Rick Britton for his thorough reading of the manuscript for historical accuracy. Any mistakes that remain are mine.

Finally, my special thanks to my editor, Emma D. Dryden, who has an exceptional eye for inconsistencies in wording and content, and found all my embarrassing errors.

CONTENTS

PREFACE

It is hard to believe, but there was a time when the United States split into two countries for four long, bloody years. North fought South, and 618,000 Americans from both sides died. This struggle was called the Civil War and it was fought over an idea called "states' rights." The North and South were very different from each other and they disagreed about several important issues. The most important disagreement involved whether people could own slaves, with many Southerners supporting slavery while many Northerners felt that no one should be allowed to own another human being. The South also felt that each state should be allowed to choose which national laws to follow, and even to withdraw from the union of states if it wanted to. The North, represented by Abraham Lincoln, strongly disagreed with this view. When Lincoln was elected president in November 1860, the South felt that it had lost. Rather than stay in the Union, the Southern states decided to secede. The Northern states were determined that the Union must be preserved at all costs. Both sides were willing to fight and die for their beliefs. And fight they did, in major battles where thousands fell and in small skirmishes. It was the saddest time in our nation's history.

But there are many interesting and exciting stories that came out of the Civil War. There are stories about armies winning in battle against hopeless odds and tales of tremendously heroic deeds of individual soldiers. Many of these stories are well known, while others are only discovered after studying the letters, diaries, and memoirs of the soldiers who fought in the Civil War. But all of them are an important part of our American heritage.

Gettysburg, more than any other Civil War battle, seems to be known for the number and quality of its stories. Perhaps this is because it is the most famous Civil War battle. Perhaps it is because of its fame as the High-Water Mark of the Confederacy. Perhaps it is because of the speech known as the Gettysburg Address, given by President Lincoln at the dedication of the Gettysburg National Cemetery four months after the battle. Whatever the reason, the Battle of Gettysburg has become a focal point in our history—a time and place that has come to symbolize an entire period of our past. The stories of this time and place are memorable ones. The story of Pickett's Charge, that hopeless trek across an open field by the Rebel soldiers in their desperate, heroic attempt to turn the tide of battle, is probably the best-known story of the three-day battle. Some of the stories are minor—the story of civilian Peter Burns, taking up his gun to defend his home, or the story of Jennie Wade, killed while baking bread. But among all the stories is one that stands out as an exceptional tale of heroism—of young men fighting bravely in the face of almost certain death, of courage far above and beyond the call of duty.

That story is about the 20th Maine Regiment and the gallant fight of Colonel Joshua Lawrence Chamberlain to hold on to his position anchoring the left end of the Union line on Little

Round Top on the afternoon of July 2, 1863, at a point when his troops were badly outnumbered and running out of ammunition. It is also the story of Colonel William Oates and his 15th Alabama Regiment, who saw a moment of opportunity to break through the Union lines and secure a Confederate victory. For a little while on the afternoon of July 2, 1863, the whole fate of the nation came down to these two leaders and their men on the slopes of Little Round Top in Gettysburg, Pennsylvania.

Here is their story. . . .

CHAPTER 1

SETTING THE SCENE

"Imagine if you can, nine small companies of infantry, numbering perhaps three hundred men, in the form of a right angle, on the extreme flank of an army of eighty thousand men, put there to hold the key of the entire position against a force at least ten times their number, and who are determined to succeed in the mission upon which they came." Private Theodore Gerrish of Maine sets the scene for the battle between the 20th Maine and the 15th Alabama. But there was much more to the battle of Little Round Top and to the war itself than this scene.

The Battle of Gettysburg was fought because the Confederate army needed shoes. At least that's the way the story is often told. In fact the Confederate army was desperate for all types of supplies.

The Civil War, by 1863, was not the war that either side had expected to fight. On that hot July day in 1861 when the Union army, followed by Washington high society in their carriages with their picnic lunches, was routed at Bull Run in Manassas, Virginia, the war that everyone had expected became one that no one had wanted. This would not be a short battle where the Confederates would make one desperate stand and then recognize the superiority of the Union and settle their differences politically. The Union army and Washington high society were sent fleeing back to Washington, and the bloody four-year conflict called the Civil War began in earnest.

Both the Union and Confederate armies learned lessons at Manassas. The volunteer soldiers from both sides spent the rest of 1861 getting ready to fight their enemies. The armies created their own flags, and uniforms that were different from each other. The Union soldiers would wear blue, the Confederates gray. That way the soldiers on the field could recognize both friend and enemy easily, even in the smoke and confusion of battle. Both armies set up medical corps since the military leaders had learned at Manassas that there would be tremendous casualties during the fighting. The men had to be trained to fight together with military discipline. Before the armies met again, these volunteers would have to learn that armies were not run democratically, with each unit—or even worse, each soldier—deciding strategy and going off to fight its own war. The battles ahead would be more organized. There could never again be the disorganized rout of Manassas from which Union soldiers straggled back to Washington as best they could.

When spring 1862 came the two armies were ready to face each other. They would fight often in skirmishes and smaller battles. But there were other engagements where they clashed in such numbers that the names of these battles would be well remembered over a hundred years later. Meeting at Shiloh, Tennessee, in April 1862, the Union army carried the battle but lost ten thousand soldiers in winning it. At the same time the Union and Confederate armies in Virginia fought back and forth, with the Union army once actually getting to within six miles of the Confederate capital in Richmond, Virginia.

But as 1862 wore on, the Confederates won their share of the battles also. In late June, it was the Union army that retreated from Richmond after the Seven Days Battle. In August, when the armies met for the second time on the fields of Manassas, the Confederates won again. The commanders of the Confederate army, made bold by their victories, decided to invade the North in order to gain a decisive victory that might bring the war to a quick conclusion. On September 17, 1862, the two armies met at Sharpsburg, Maryland, on Antietam Creek, in fighting that gave us the bloodiest day in our history, with over twenty-three thousand soldiers killed or wounded on both sides. This time the retreat was by the Confederate army, and it moved back into Virginia.

Before the year was finished, the two armies would meet one more time in a major battle, at Fredericksburg, Virginia. In December 1862 the Union army would be the one retreating. The two armies settled in for the winter, facing each other halfway between the Union capital in Washington and the Confederate capital in Richmond.

Fredericksburg was one of the rare major Civil War battles fought in the winter months. The cold, rainy or snowy weather—and even worse roads—made winter fighting almost impossible. The two armies built permanent camps, not that far away from each other, and spent the winter preparing for the spring campaigns. The soldiers often used their summer tents as roofs on new huts that they built for themselves out of logs. They even built simple fireplaces to heat their winter homes. Soldiers on both sides took great pride in their winter quarters and gave them fancy names and wrote home describing the huts in great detail.

Spring 1863 found the two armies fighting each other again.

Two Union soldiers posing in uniform with their muskets and equipment.

In early May they met at Chancellorsville, Virginia, and the Confederate army won a major victory. General Robert E. Lee, in command of the Confederate Army of Northern Virginia, made the decision to invade the North again, in part so that his army could get the supplies it needed. He started moving his units slowly northwest and then wrote to Confederate Secretary of War James Seddon on June 8, "As far as I can judge, there is nothing to be gained by this army remaining quietly on the defensive. . . . I am aware that there is difficulty and hazard in taking the aggressive . . . still, I think it is worth a trial." Seddon wrote back, agreeing with General Lee that "such action is indispensable to our safety and independence, and all attendant sacrifices and risks must be incurred." By the middle of June the Confederate army of seventy thousand men was on the march north through the Shenandoah Valley of Virginia. Leaving Confederate soil, they continued their march through West Virginia and Maryland and on into Pennsylvania.

Now that the decision was made, General Lee started giving orders about obtaining supplies. Two years of fighting in Virginia had made it nearly impossible to provide for the needs of the army while it remained in the area. Lee hoped to get his army resupplied in Maryland and Pennsylvania before coming up against the Union Army of the Potomac. He also wanted to do this without angering the civilians in the areas the army would be going through. The North had the supplies, but Lee wasn't trying to steal from the Union civilians. The Confederates were willing to buy what they needed. Lee cautioned his officers to take only what was necessary and "give receipts to the owners, stating the kind, quantity, and estimated value of the articles received." But he also made it clear that

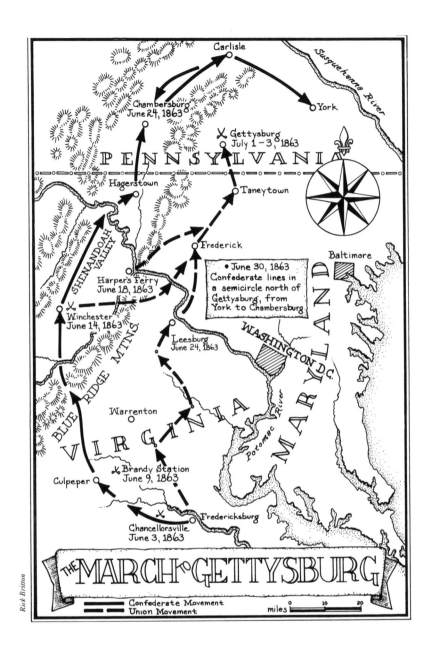

Carlisle

Susquehanna River

Chambersburg
June 24, 1863

York

✗ Gettysburg
July 1–3, 1863

P E N N S Y L V A N I A

Hagerstown

Taneytown

SHENANDOAH VALLEY

Frederick

Baltimore

Harper's Ferry
June 18, 1863

• June 30, 1863
Confederate lines in
a semicircle north of
Gettysburg, from
York to Chambersburg

✗ Winchester
June 14, 1863

BLUE RIDGE MTNS.

Leesburg
June 24, 1863

WASHINGTON D.C.

M A R Y L A N D

Potomac River

Warrenton

V I R G I N I A

✗ Brandy Station
June 9, 1863

Culpeper

✗ Fredericksburg

Chancellorsville
June 3, 1863

THE MARCH to GETTYSBURG

Rick Britton

▬▬▬▬ Confederate Movement
▬ ▬ ▬ Union Movement

miles 0   10   20

18

if the Union citizens would not sell to them, his soldiers could take what they needed. Letter after letter to his officers told them to "collect all the supplies you can for use of the army."

As his army entered Pennsylvania in late June, Lee found the supplies he needed. On July 1 he ordered General John D. Imboden to "obtain all the flour that you can load in your wagons from the mills in your vicinity, and if you cannot get sufficient, I believe there are 700 or 800 barrels at Shippensburg." General Imboden was also to control a critical road leading into a small town called Gettysburg while "getting everything prepared for active operations in the field."

Lee had his army spread out in a wide arc centered around Chambersburg, Pennsylvania. Some parts of the army had moved north to Carlisle. Some were as far east as York. Lee had sent out General J. E. B. Stuart with the main body of the Confederate cavalry to locate the main part of the Union army, but Stuart had not yet returned. Lee decided to tighten up his command and, on June 29 and 30, he brought his troops into a thirty-mile-long line around Cashtown and Gettysburg. Lee didn't know that his army was about to meet the Union army. He would not have time to complete his plans for resupplying his soldiers.

The Union Army of the Potomac was very close by. After their defeat at Chancellorsville, the Union soldiers were regrouped, facing their enemy across the Rappahannock River. From this position, the soldiers began to see some movement of Confederate troops. On June 3 Union force commander General Joseph Hooker had received an intelligence report that "this movement of General Lee's is not intended to menace Washington, but to try his hand again toward Maryland."

On June 4 there was hard evidence that at least some of the Confederate units were on the move. Major General Daniel Butterfield, Chief of Staff of the Union Army of the Potomac, reported, "Reports and appearances here indicate the disappearance of a portion of the enemy's forces from opposite our left." His orders were "to keep a sharp lookout, country well scouted, and advise us as soon as possible of anything in your front or vicinity indicating a movement." The next day Butterfield reported to Major General George Gordon Meade, "The enemy appears to have moved the greater part of his forces from our front. . . . We cannot tell where they have moved to."

By June 13 Butterfield had more of an idea where the Confederate army was headed: "It is probable that a movement is on foot to turn our right or go into Maryland." President Lincoln was concerned about this threatened invasion of Northern soil. On June 15 he ordered the militia units from the states of Maryland, Pennsylvania, Ohio, and West Virginia transferred to the command of the Union army for the next six months.

It was a confused time for the Union leadership. Reading over the reports contained in the official records, it is clear that General Hooker did not know where he should be. Reports were arriving every day that claimed to be accurate. But the reports contradicted one another. One report even claimed that the majority of the Confederate Army of Northern Virginia had been sent out west to help in the siege of Vicksburg, Mississippi, over eight hundred fifty miles away.

For General Hooker, a cautious man who wanted definite answers before taking action, it must have been a nerve-racking time. He was, in fact, doing an adequate job keeping up with the Confederate army and preventing it from being a threat to Washington. By late June the Union army was just over the Pennsylvania line in Maryland, about twenty miles west of Frederick. General Hooker had brought it to where it would be able to cut the Confederate army off from supplies and retreat, but he was unwilling to do anything more, especially to attack the army that had beaten him so badly the month before.

As the people of the area complained more and more about the invasion of the Confederate army onto Northern soil, Lincoln replaced General Hooker with General Meade on June 28 because Hooker was not aggressive enough when he faced General Lee in battle. Meade had a reputation as a very solid, competent, professional soldier who would not be intimidated in fighting General Lee.

Meade went right to work. He would set up a good defensive position along Pipe Creek in Maryland and move the army slowly forward (north) until it encountered the Confederate army. As Lee wrote his orders to Imboden on July 1, he did not know that later that day the Union and Confederate armies would meet in the first fight of the most famous battle in American history. Here the Civil War would be won or lost, even though its end was almost two years away. Neither army was really ready for the battle that would take place in the small town of Gettysburg, Pennsylvania, over the next few days.

CHAPTER 2

TWO LIVES BEFORE THE WAR

In some ways they were so alike, the two colonels who would face each other on Little Round Top at Gettysburg. There would be many parts of their later lives that paralleled each other. In other ways they could not have been more different.

"I make no pretense to scholarly attainments, nor did I ever have the advantages of a classical education," William Calvin Oates would write in the preface to his memoirs. Born December 1, 1835, in Pike County, Alabama, he was seven years younger than his opponent on that hill in Gettysburg. He had also had a much rougher childhood and early adult life. His father was a planter, and Oates attended school near home as a young child. But at sixteen he left that home and for the next several years he was a wanderer, famous more for getting into fights and for gambling than for anything else.

Eventually Oates returned home and taught school in Henry County, Alabama, while he studied the law books provided by a local law firm. He passed the bar exam and began practicing law in Abbeville, Alabama, in 1859. He also served as editor of a local newspaper. He was now settled in and his career was doing well. Then, when Oates was twenty-five, the event began that would change his life and that of hundreds of thousands of other young men forever. The Southern states seceded from the Union, and Oates never hesitated. Since he was still unmarried, there was nothing to hold him back from this great adventure. Years later Oates wrote proudly of his own service and that of other soldiers fighting for the Confederacy. He noted that all of them "were terribly in earnest and were stimulated by the highest patriotism to maintain their God-given right to govern themselves and their own state institutions." Being a soldier would be an adventure. It would also be a chance to prove his love and devotion to the South. The Civil War would bring Oates to Little Round Top on the afternoon of July 2, 1863, and life would never be the same for him again.

Joshua Lawrence Chamberlain came to adulthood and to the war a very different person from Oates. Born Lawrence Joshua Chamberlain on September 8, 1828, in Brewer, Maine, he grew up happily in a home where education was highly valued. He was an excellent student. His father hoped to see him train at West Point for a military career. His mother wanted him to become a minister. In 1848 he became a student at Bowdoin College in Brunswick, Maine, and there found the area he wanted to study—language and rhetoric (public speaking). He won prizes in speaking and in writing and, when he graduated, was selected to give the "First Class Oration," a sort of valedictorian's speech.

While still a student, Chamberlain also met his future wife. They became engaged in 1852, but then Frances Caroline Adams, known as Fanny, went off to teach voice and music at a girls' school in Georgia, while Chamberlain became a student at Bangor Theological Seminary. Three years later, Fanny

Colonel William Calvin Oates in 1864.

returned to Maine. Chamberlain had just graduated and was to begin teaching at Bowdoin College in the fall. On December 7, 1855, he and Fanny were married.

In 1856 Chamberlain was appointed professor of rhetoric and oratory at Bowdoin, and in October their first child was born. Now signing his papers Joshua L. Chamberlain, he had found his calling in life. Happily married, he would be a successful college professor.

In 1861, when the Civil War began, Chamberlain was ready to wait out what everyone thought would be a short war. But over time his desire to fight grew stronger. He was due to leave Bowdoin for a two-year sabbatical to travel in Europe as part of his promotion to head of the language department at the college, but in July 1862 Chamberlain decided instead to go and fight for the Union. No one was pleased with this decision. The board of the college was furious, his father was opposed to the war, and Fanny was angry at being left with their two children and no support if something happened to him.

Unlike Oates, Chamberlain did have other obligations that would have justified a decision to stay at home. But, like Oates, nothing would keep him back from this great adventure. Chamberlain, as Oates had for the South, felt the need to fight to defend his belief in the Northern cause. In offering his services to the governor of Maine, he wrote that the war "will not cease until the men of the North are willing to leave good positions, and sacrifice the dearest personal interests, to rescue our Country." For Chamberlain, too, the events on Little Round Top on July 2 would change his life forever.

The war would bring these two men together in battle. But it would also bring their lives following the war together. Both would leave this war with permanent injuries. Both would go on to lead lives as public men. Joshua Lawrence Chamberlain would become governor of Maine. William Calvin Oates would be governor of Alabama. The two men, so very different in their youths, would emerge from the trials of the Civil War more alike and destined to mirror each other's careers in later life.

Joshua Lawrence Chamberlain as a major general.

CHAPTER 3

COMING TO GETTYSBURG
THE 15TH ALABAMA

William Calvin Oates was ready to fight for his home state of Alabama from the very beginning of the Civil War. At first he organized a company of men from Henry County, in the southeastern part of the state, to serve for one year, but the governor refused to accept it because he was more interested in forming larger units of soldiers for long-term service. Oates returned home and disbanded his company, and "the day it disbanded I began the work of raising a company to serve three years or during the war." His timing was right, and this company became part of the 15th Alabama Infantry Regiment, which was being organized by a wealthy planter named James Canty, who lived in Russell County, about seventy miles away from Oates's home.

The company, with Oates as its captain "by common consent," left Abbeville for Fort Mitchell in Russell County on Saturday, July 27, 1861. There were 121 soldiers, including Captain Oates. He described these volunteers as sons of farmers, most between sixteen and thirty years old, with only four of them older than forty. Thirteen of them were married. All of them were committed to fighting for three years or until the war ended. Oates's men would make up Company G of the

15th Alabama, 120 men out of 1,033 in the entire regiment.

When they arrived at Fort Mitchell in Russell County, the men were given their weapons. But rifles were scarce, and only two of the eleven companies in the 15th Alabama could have the new rifles. Company G was given "old altered smooth-bore George Law muskets." With weapons in hand, the work of turning these volunteers into soldiers began. Oates remembered it this way: "Volunteers, who scarcely knew right face from left face and had never seen a company drilled through a single evolution, could not have been otherwise; but when the officers were found to be nearly, if not quite, as ignorant as the men they were attempting to instruct . . . the whole thing presented a ludicrous scene."

In August the 15th Alabama began its move to Richmond, Virginia, traveling by train two companies at a time. Oates describes all the material they had to take with them: "Ten large tents, ten large mess-chests—each one supplied with enough crockery, cutlery and tinware to furnish ten family dining-rooms—a large quantity of cooking utensils, a dozen trunks filled with clothing, and a large quantity of blankets. . . . The baggage of my company was all that could be packed on a large four-horse army wagon." With their equipment packed, the volunteers boarded the train and the young men "cheered lustily."

They arrived in a Richmond that was sure the war would be won by the Confederate army. The Confederate rout of the Union troops at Manassas had given the Southerners a great feeling of self-confidence. The 15th Alabama camped outside Richmond and began drilling as part of a brigade. Within a few weeks the men were ordered to move again, this time to the

Confederate front lines at Manassas Junction. They camped about a mile east of where the battle had occurred. Oates was quick to visit the scene of the Confederate victory, but what he saw there was not what he had expected: "Some of the mounds where the slain were buried were washed down by the rains until here and there could be discovered a putrifying human hand or foot protruding. . . . The mashed and bruised weeds still gave forth a peculiar odor, which some of the men who visited the field superstitiously mistook for the scent of 'dead Yankees', supposing that they had a different smell from other dead men."

There was no Union army for the troops to fight for the rest of 1861, but the regiment instead waged a battle against measles, which Oates called "that worst enemy of our army." Oates watched as whole units came down with the dread disease. Writing forty years later, Oates was still bitter that his men suffered so much from this disease because of camp conditions: "Everything else should have been subordinated to their [the soldiers'] comfort and preservation; but on the contrary they were neglected and a large percentage lost by disease."

The numbers show that Oates was right. Of the 618,000 soldiers from both sides who died during the Civil War, only 200,000 died from wounds they received in battle. The other deaths were all from diseases like measles, diarrhea, and pneumonia. The soldiers on both sides ate food that was bad, lived in overcrowded camps where disease could spread quickly, and didn't keep themselves very clean. Dr. Roberts Bartholow, a Union surgeon, described the problem very well. He said that so many soldiers died from disease because the new soldier was "supplied with army rations badly cooked and uncleanly served . . . furnished with one or two blankets . . . thrust into a tent with a large number of others" often in places that were cold and damp. The soldier was also "required to perform a tour of guard duty which interrupts his habit of nightly repose" and at the same time was given "slender opportunities of washing and bathing," while being exposed to "the emanations from his comrades suffering from various contagious maladies." So Oates had a right to be bitter. That soldiers on both sides survived camp life with enough energy left to fight each other was extraordinary.

Those who survived that first winter in camp had a busy year beginning the following spring. The 15th Alabama was assigned to General Stonewall Jackson's army, taking part in the Battle of Winchester and in Jackson's 1862 Shenandoah Valley campaign. Now they were involved in fighting a real enemy. In June they fought in the Seven Days Battle outside Richmond and then in Second Manassas in August. Here Oates discovered "two men several steps in the rear of our line lying as close to the ground on their faces as ever a frightened squirrel lay upon the branch of a tree. They did not move until I used the flat side of my sword very freely upon their backs." Oates would see to it that his company of the 15th Alabama became a seasoned fighting unit.

On September 17, 1862, the 15th Alabama found itself in the thick of the fighting in the East Wood and Cornfield at Antietam Creek in Sharpsburg, Maryland. Caught in a cross fire between two Union units, one part of Trimble's Brigade (which included the 15th Alabama) left sixty of their one hundred men on the field. It was in the reorganization after the

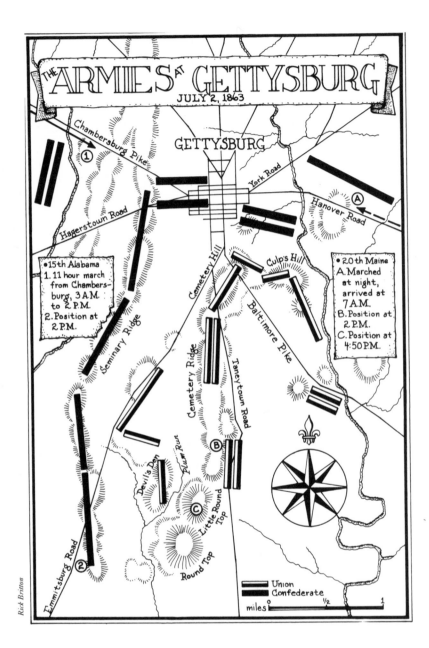

THE ARMIES AT GETTYSBURG
JULY 2, 1863

GETTYSBURG

Chambersburg Pike

①

York Road

Hagerstown Road

Hanover Road

Ⓐ

Culp's Hill

Cemetery Hill

• 15th Alabama
1. 11 hour march
from Chambers-
burg, 3 A.M.
to 2 P.M.
2. Position at
2 P.M.

• 20th Maine
A. Marched
at night,
arrived at
7 A.M.
B. Position at
2 P.M.
C. Position at
4:50 P.M.

Seminary Ridge

Cemetery Ridge

Baltimore Pike

Taneytown Road

Ⓑ

Plum Run

Devil's Den

Ⓒ

Little Round Top

Emmitsburg Road

②

Round Top

▬▬ Union
▬▬ Confederate
miles 0   ½   1

Rick Britton

32

battle at Antietam that Oates was given command of the 15th Alabama.

At Fredericksburg, Virginia, in December, Oates's men found themselves in the thick of the fighting on Marye's Heights. Oates would remember the soldiers lying there "right under the muzzles of the guns, and the Federals replying with thirty-seven pieces, which made the position of the Fifteenth as perilous and disagreeable as well could be."

The following spring the 15th Alabama, led by the newly promoted Colonel William C. Oates, was transferred from Jackson's Corps to Lieutenant General James Longstreet's Corps and fought in the Battle of Chancellorsville in May. Victory there put the Confederate army, including the 15th Alabama, on the march north, where the Alabamians would have their fateful meeting with the 20th Maine on Thursday, July 2, on the hill called Little Round Top.

CHAPTER 4

COMING TO GETTYSBURG
THE 20TH MAINE

No one looking at the new unit known as the 20th Maine would have believed it was destined for such glory. The Union unit that would earn such tremendous praise for its stand at Little Round Top would not have been recognized by someone looking at it just ten months earlier, when the regiment was first formed. The 20th Maine was formed, under the command of Colonel Adelbert Ames, at Camp Mason, near Portland, Maine, on August 29, 1862. The unit was marched from Portland to Boston, Massachusetts, and then transported by ship to Alexandria, Virginia, arriving on September 7. At this point, the men had no training and hadn't even been issued their rifles. After they received their equipment, their first orders were to march to join Colonel T. B. W. Stockton's Third Brigade on its way to Maryland. The result was chaos.

Private Theodore Gerrish, one of these new soldiers in the 20th Maine, remembered his first march this way: "It was a most ludicrous march. We had never been drilled, and we felt our reputation was at stake. An untrained drum corps furnished us with music; each musician kept different time, and each man in the regiment took a different step. Old soldiers sneered; the people laughed and cheered; we marched, ran, walked, galloped, and stood still, in our vain endeavor to keep

Soldiers lining up for a meal in camp. Conditions in camp varied according to the location of the camp and the time of year. As a rule, the Union camps were better organized and better supplied than the Confederate ones. But camp life on both sides was marked by disease, spoiled food, and damp and unhealthy living quarters.

step." Most of them couldn't even keep up the pace. When the 20th Maine rested for the night, many members were still scrambling to catch up. It was not the most glorious start for any unit to make.

The 20th Maine joined General Fitz John Porter's Corps at the Battle of Antietam in Maryland, just ten days after its arrival in Virginia. Fortunately the men were not asked to fight, but instead served as a reserve unit. Some of the men crawled to the top of a hill and watched the action taking place on the fields below. The 20th was sent to follow the Confederate army as it retreated from Maryland. The brigade came under heavy fire when it crossed the Potomac River at Shepherdstown and got too close to the retreating army. No one was injured as the 20th retreated back to safety on the Maryland side of the river.

For the next several months, the 20th Maine worked at becoming a fighting unit, learning the drill and instruction needed to fight well within the larger army. At the same time, the men went through the normal sicknesses of new units in the army. Private Gerrish had a bad case of typhoid fever, not at all unusual for soldiers adjusting themselves to the dirty camp conditions. This shaping-up period was important for the new recruits. It forced them to either become tougher or to drop out. By the time they faced their enemy for the first time in battle, these men would be ready to act like real soldiers.

To turn these volunteers into soldiers required the right kind of leadership. In Joshua Lawrence Chamberlain, the Maine volunteers were lucky. Chamberlain proved to be an effective leader of his men. At one point, when Chamberlain was being recommended for a promotion, his commanding officer, Brigadier General James C. Rice, listed the leadership qualities he showed: "My personal knowledge of this gallant officer's skill and bravery upon the battle field, his ability in drill and discipline, and his fidelity to duty in camp, added to a just admiration for his scholarship, and respect for his Christian Character induces me to ask your influence in his behalf." Another soldier (not from the 20th Maine) wrote to Chamberlain many years after the war, telling him, "Nineteen Years ago today . . . You Struck me with the Flat of Your Sword. But not in Anger but to arrest my attention as I in common with the rest of the 1st Brigade was doing some tall running." It is a reflection on Chamberlain's leadership that he was able to train his men to be good soldiers without having them hate him.

The first battle of the newly drilled 20th Maine was not long in coming. At Fredericksburg, Virginia, in December 1862, the regiment was sent in to relieve the front lines of Union troops. In the words of Private Gerrish, the men spent the next two days "flat in the mud upon our faces, to escape the shells that were screaming and crashing over our heads. . . . The air was filled with iron hail." Gerrish spoke proudly of how the soldiers held up under the strain of battle, saying, "We had fought our first battle, had made a most brilliant charge with unbroken ranks, where veteran regiments had faltered in fear." It would not be their last or most glorious charge. But now they knew that they could stand the heat of battle.

Huddled on the battlefield after their charge through the cold December night at the very front of the Union line, the men of the 20th Maine used the dead bodies on the field as protection from the bitterly frigid wind. Chamberlain would write that for that night "the living and the dead were alike to me." It was the sound of the night he would remember most—

the sound of the moans of the wounded mixed with the wind. He called it "weird, unearthly, terrible to hear and bear." The 20th Maine, withdrawn from the lines after two days, now knew what it was like to fight and to see the dead and dying on the field around them. The men would be prepared when they came to Gettysburg on a very hot day the following July.

After the battle at Fredericksburg, the 20th Maine returned to its original camp near Stoneman's Switch, Virginia, for the winter. Except for a few reconnaissance trips to find out what the enemy was doing, the soldiers remained there all winter. In April 1863, when the spring campaigns began, the 20th Maine was assigned to guard the telegraph lines while the battle at Chancellorsville was under way. The men were fairly safe there, although they did come under some enemy artillery fire. Colonel Ames was promoted to brigadier general after that battle, and his second in command, Lieutenant Colonel Joshua L. Chamberlain, was put in charge of the regiment.

The unit was ordered to march northwest beginning in late May. They spent most of their time marching, but they did come up against two brigades of Confederate cavalry near Upperville, Virginia. The 20th Maine was victorious in the skirmish that followed, although one man was killed and several others were wounded. Continuing their march, on July 2, the 20th Maine arrived in Gettysburg, Pennsylvania, where a fierce battle had begun the day before.

Little did these men know, as they took their place at the far left end of the Union line, that this day would be their day of glory and that, after today, the 20th Maine, although much smaller in number, would earn the reputation as one of the bravest fighting units in American history.

CHAPTER 5

GETTYSBURG

THE EARLY PART OF THE BATTLE

The battle of Gettysburg—which would be known as the High-Water Mark of the Confederacy—began with a skirmish at four-thirty in the morning on July 1 on the Chambersburg Pike. Confederate General Pettigrew's men were on the march into Gettysburg to get supplies, but along the way they encountered a Union cavalry unit. The Confederates advanced slowly, pushing the unit back toward Gettysburg, thinking they were fighting a small local militia unit.

The Union leaders rushed troops to defend the area, and suddenly the Confederate leaders realized that they had come upon part of the Union Army of the Potomac. Both armies scrambled to bring in more men to send against each other.

It was not a good morning for the surprised Confederates. Hundreds of their troops were taken prisoner by morning's end. The Union army was holding a hill called McPherson's Ridge, just northwest of the town of Gettysburg. The Confederates stopped their attack, and in the early afternoon there was an uneasy calm on the field.

General Lee had given orders earlier that his troops were not to push against Union troops and cause a general battle to begin. He needed time to complete the concentration of his army in one position. But General A. P. Hill, who was in command of Lee's Third Corps, decided not to wait. With General Ewell's Second Corps, the Confederates moved into position and began an attack on the Union troops at about two-thirty in the afternoon.

At this early stage of the battle, there were far more Confederate troops on the field than Union troops. By four o'clock the Confederate troops were driving the outnumbered Union troops back from McPherson's Ridge to Seminary Ridge, back through the town of Gettysburg and onto Cemetery Ridge.

For the Confederates this day was a victory. But it had been a hard fight, and eight thousand Confederate soldiers were killed or wounded. The Union army lost twelve thousand men, but reinforcements were almost at Gettysburg. The Union was left in a very good defensive position on Cemetery Ridge and Culp's Hill, although they were outnumbered by the Confederates. A determined Confederate attack that evening might have broken through the Union lines.

But the Confederate leaders decided to wait until the next day to stage their attack. By morning, their chance at a quick victory would have passed. That night the two armies maneuvered for position. By the time the fighting began on the afternoon of July 2, the Union would have seventy thousand men and three hundred fifty cannons on the field against Lee's fifty thousand men and two hundred cannons. As July 1 ended, it seemed inevitable that the big clash of armies would begin the next day.

The 15th Alabama had spent July 1 on picket duty near New Guilford Court House east of Chambersburg. Although twenty-five miles away from the fighting, Oates would remember that "the cannonading of the engagement . . . was distinctly heard by us." That evening Oates received orders. His men were to cook rations and be ready to march by three the next morning. They would not arrive at Gettysburg, after their "rapid and fatiguing march," until two o'clock on the afternoon of July 2.

The 20th Maine had also missed the fighting on July 1. The regiment was marching north from Maryland into Pennsylvania on that day and could also hear the guns in the distance. The men camped near Hanover at about five o'clock and were just settling down to supper when a messenger arrived telling Chamberlain of the day's fight and ordering his men to march quickly to Gettysburg, sixteen miles away. They marched until midnight and then slept by the side of the road for a few hours. Private Gerrish remembered that march as almost magical: "Night came on but we halted not. We knew that our comrades on the distant battle-field needed our aid and we hastened on. It was a beautiful evening. The moon shone from a cloudless sky and flooded our way with its glorious light. . . . That moonlight march will always be remembered by its survivors." For many of the soldiers of the 20th Maine it would be the last night of their young lives.

As morning dawned they marched the last few miles to Gettysburg, arriving at about seven. Exhausted and hungry, they were placed in position on Cemetery Ridge. Several times their position was moved, and in between moves they tried to get some food and some rest.

While the 15th Alabama and the 20th Maine were marching into their final battle positions, the generals on both sides were making decisions that would determine where and when the two units would meet in battle. General Lee decided to have James Longstreet's Corps attack Big and Little Round Tops at the left end of the Union line. The 15th Alabama was one small part of that corps—a group of five Alabama units that made up General Law's Brigade. The Union leaders, watching the movements of the Confederate army, decided to check out their position on the Round Tops. General Meade sent his engineer, General Gouverneur Warren, to survey the area. Warren was shocked to find almost no Union troops on Little Round Top and none on Big Round Top. He ordered part of Major General George Sykes's 5th Army Corps to quickly occupy Little Round Top and hold it against the enemy.

Sykes ordered the 1st Division to the hill, but his messenger could not find the 1st Division leader. All that could be done was to send one small brigade of thirteen hundred men under the command of Colonel Strong Vincent to stop the advancing Confederate army. Colonel Vincent's men—the 20th Maine, the 16th Michigan, the 44th New York, and the 83rd Pennsylvania—hurried into positions at the top of Little Round Top. Their moment in history was about to begin.

W. *Michael Beller*

A statue of General Gouverneur Warren now stands on the peak of Little Round Top where he stood on July 2, 1863, and spotted Confederate troops hurrying to attack this unguarded position.

CHAPTER 6

THE BATTLE
OPPORTUNITY LOST FOR
THE CONFEDERATES

The 15th Alabama, along with the rest of General Law's Brigade, had marched twenty-eight miles in eleven hours in a forced march at a fast pace, with no time to stop for a rest along the way. A forced march was very hard on the soldiers and was used only when the officers felt it was critical that a unit arrive at the battlefield as soon as possible.

Now they were beginning their advance across the field. General Law pulled the 48th Alabama from the line of march to help a Texas unit under fire at Devil's Den. The 15th was left to hold the entire right side of the line by itself.

As the men reached the base of the hill, they began their climb up Little Round Top, trying to drive back the Union sharpshooters, who had been plaguing their march. Oates wrote, "In places the men had to climb up, catching to the rocks and bushes and crawling over the boulders in the face of the fire of the enemy, who kept retreating, taking shelter, and firing down on us from behind the rocks and crags which covered the side of the mountain thicker than grave-stones in a city cemetery." It was a grueling climb for the 15th Alabama. The men were out of water, it was an extremely hot day, and Oates later remembered that "some of my men fainted from heat, exhaustion, and thirst."

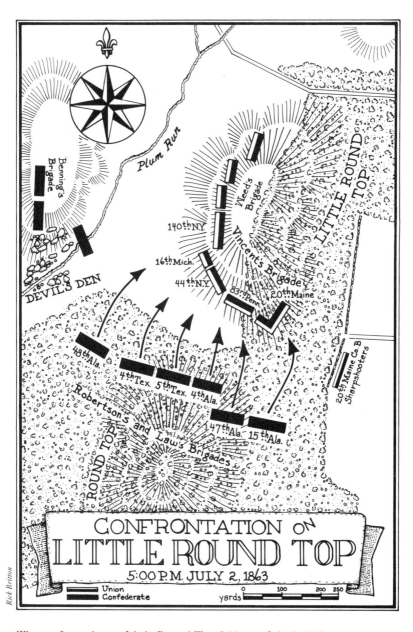

The confrontation on Little Round Top 5:00 p.m. July 2, 1863.

Oates's younger brother, John, a lieutenant, had fallen behind in the forced march. Colonel Oates "sent back a horse for him and he came up. Just before we advanced I went to him where he was lying on the ground in [the] rear of his company, and saw at once that he was sick." Oates told him to stay behind as he was too ill to fight, but John insisted on moving forward with his men when they marched.

Oates knew his men needed a few minutes of rest before continuing. He named two men from each of his eleven companies to collect all the canteens and fill them at a well they had passed. The canteen detail left, but General Law's orders to march came before they returned.

Years later, Oates bitterly remembered: "It would have been infinitely better to have waited five minutes for those twenty-two men and the canteens of water, but generals never ask a colonel if his regiment is ready to move." The water would never reach the men. The canteen detail could not find them when they returned. They ended up walking right into Union lines and were taken prisoner, "canteens and all." Oates would blame the lack of water and the absence of the twenty-two men for "our failure to take Little Round Top a few minutes later." What a very small detail to effect the outcome of an entire battle.

But this was a minor disappointment for Oates compared to what happened next. While his men had been resting, waiting for water, Oates had been observing the area around them. They were between two hills, Big and Little Round Top. The Union troops were scrambling to protect Little Round Top as the Confederate army advanced. But Oates saw an even more important opportunity for the Confederates. As Captain

The Gettysburg battlefield. Little Round Top is to the left, Big Round Top to the right.

Terrell, General Law's aide, came with orders to march imme-
diately, Oates pointed out to him the larger hill, telling him
that "within half an hour I could convert it into a Gibraltar that
I could hold against ten times the number of men that I had."
Terrell agreed, but would not authorize a change in General
Law's order.

Oates was frustrated. Terrell did not know where General
Law was and was insisting that Oates follow the original orders.
Oates would write, "I felt confident that Law did not know my
position, or he would not order me from it." But Oates "consid-
ered it my duty to obey the orders" and reluctantly he turned
away from Big Round Top. He would remember that decision
later with much regret, convinced that he had given up "the
key point of the field, as artillery on it would have commanded
the other Round Top and the Federal line toward Gettysburg
as far as it extended along Cemetery Ridge."

As Major General John Bell Hood's Division moved into
position against Little Round Top at four-thirty, Law's Brigade
lined up to attack from the southwest, up the side of Little
Round Top. In a row, running from left to right, were the 4th
and 5th Texas of Robertson's Brigade and then Law's 4th
Alabama, 47th Alabama, and finally, at the far right end, the
15th Alabama, under Oates's command.

The left end of the line came into contact with the enemy
first, coming up against the 16th Michigan, the 44th New York,
and the 83rd Pennsylvania. The fighting was furious and
the Confederates drove the Union units back, pushing them
from their position halfway up the hill all the way to the crest.

Meanwhile, Oates moved the 15th Alabama into position to

Taken shortly after the battle, this shows the side of the wall facing the Confederates as they charged up the front of Little Round Top. Many Confederate soldiers died trying to break through this position. Many Union soldiers died defending it.

march on the far right side of Little Round Top, arriving on the hill only ten minutes after Colonel Vincent's four Union regiments had scrambled into position to hold the crest. There Oates met with "the most destructive fire I ever saw." Oates and his men continued their advance while also turning slightly to the right in an attempt to turn the side of the 20th Maine's line.

Wherever they went, it seemed the Maine men were there first. One of the men of the 20th Maine, Captain Howard L. Prince, would later describe this attack by Oates and his men: "At times the hostile forces were actually at hand-to-hand distance. Twice the rebels were followed down the slope so sharply that they were obliged to use the bayonet, and in places small squads of their men in their charges reached our actual front." Driven back, the Alabamians charged again and, as Oates later wrote, "advanced about half way to the enemy's position but the fire was so destructive that my line wavered like a man trying to walk against a strong wind.... To stand there and die was sheer folly; either to retreat or advance became a necessity."

Oates called, "Forward, men, to the ledge!" and his men advanced again. The Maine men and the Alabama men moved back and forth on the side of the small hill. Oates remembered five separate charges and then his men breaching the makeshift rock walls of the Maine regiment.

But the 15th Alabama had gotten separated from the rest of the Confederate line and was under attack by Union troops on two sides. They could not hold the line; Oates's position "rapidly became untenable ... With a withering and deadly fire

The same scene as in the preceding picture, photographed today. The white marker in front of the wall shows the area defended by the Union brigade of which the 20th Maine was a part. Just beyond the fence on the right is a small monument marking the spot where Colonel Strong Vincent, the brigade commander, died during the fighting. His last orders to Chamberlain were, "To hold this ground at all costs."

W. Michael Beller

51

pouring in upon us from every direction, it seemed that the regiment was doomed to destruction." Oates had no choice. When the next charge of the 20th Maine had been held off and there was a moment of pause in the battle, he ordered a retreat. The men responded immediately, and "ran like a herd of cattle."

The men of the 15th Alabama stumbled back down the hill. Oates tried to regroup the regiment, but the men were too scattered. Oates himself, "overcome by heat and exertion . . . fainted and fell." Two of his soldiers carried him to safety so that he would not be taken prisoner by the Union troops following them down the hill. For the 15th Alabama, now with only a little more than half of the four hundred soldiers they had begun the fight with, the day had been an opportunity lost, a day that Oates would remember bitterly, even forty years later when he wrote his memoirs.

For the rest of the Alabamians and the Texans in Robertson's Brigade, the end of the day's fighting was the same. Their early progress up the face of Little Round Top had been stopped. Suddenly they found themselves facing fifteen hundred fresh soldiers as reserve troops were called in against them. It was too much for the exhausted Confederates, and they were forced back down the slope.

CHAPTER 7
THE BATTLE
OPPORTUNITY GAINED FOR THE UNION

In his memoir Private Gerrish captured the intensity of the battle between the 20th Maine and the 15th Alabama on that hot July 2 at Gettysburg. "We were on the left of our brigade and consequently on the extreme left of all our line of battle. The ground sloped to our front and left, and was sparsely covered with a growth of oak trees, which were too small to afford us any protection. Shells were crashing through the air above our heads, making so much noise that we could hardly hear the commands of our officers; the air was filled with fragments of exploding shells and splinters torn from mangled trees."

The 20th Maine would earn its place in history on that afternoon, but in some ways it was only because someone made a mistake. When Union General Meade ordered his army into position, the men were formed in a fishhook, with the straight side along Cemetery Ridge. It was only in the afternoon when the Union leaders saw the Confederates coming at them from the south at an angle that they realized the Confederates might be planning to outflank them rather than come at them straight on. General Meade sent General Gouverneur Warren to survey the area. Warren saw something very similar to what Colonel Oates of Alabama would notice later in the afternoon. An army that could take the Round Tops could control the whole line of Cemetery Ridge.

It was Colonel Strong Vincent's Brigade of four regiments that was sent scrambling into position to cover the side of the Union lines. From the crest of Little Round Top the soldiers made a right-angle turn to stop any Confederate advance up the side of the hill. The 20th Maine was given the farthest end of the Union line, making them responsible for stopping any Confederate attempt to cut around in back of the Union army. It could be a very important position, and the 20th Maine arrived to defend it only a short time before Colonel Oates and his 15th Alabama made their first attack up the slope.

Colonel Chamberlain's 20th Maine was the least experienced of the four units, and Colonel Vincent felt it was best placed at the end of the Union line. He felt that the heaviest attack would come right at the point where the Union line made a right angle at the crest of Little Round Top. At first this was what happened. The oncoming Confederate troops drove the 16th Michigan back, breaching their lines. The 44th New York bent its line back on itself as it found itself facing Confederate fire below and from the side. All their last-minute scrambling for position on the hill might well be in vain.

In their position at the end of the line, the 20th Maine used loose rocks to build a rough wall of sorts among the large boulders already on the hill. As the Confederates attacked, the worst fire came against the other units in the line, as Vincent had expected. Then Colonel Oates and the Alabamians arrived on the battlefield. Oates wanted to get to the other side of the 20th Maine so that his men could enfilade, or shoot right down the lines. It was an ambitious goal, but one he just might have been able to achieve. It was very important that Chamberlain

The line held by the 20th Maine was actually very short. The marker on the right indicates the right end of the line. To the far left, hidden in the trees, is the 20th Maine monument, marking the left end of the line. As the 15th Alabama attacked over and over again, 358 Maine soldiers crouched behind this makeshift stone wall.

W. Michael Beller

55

and his 20th Maine prevent that from happening, because if it did occur, the Confederates would have an opportunity to turn the entire Union line.

Like Colonel Oates earlier on Big Round Top, Colonel Chamberlain was a good judge of the terrain around him and of the possible uses of the terrain by his enemy. He detached one company of his men and sent them to the far left, about five hundred feet beyond the end of his line: "I immediately detached Company B, Captain Morrill commanding, to extend my left flank across this hollow as a line of skirmishers, with directions to act as occasion might dictate, to prevent a surprise on my exposed flank and rear." Chamberlain realized that now, even if the enemy did turn his line, the Confederates would find themselves with this company at their backs. It was a clever way to deploy his troops.

Chamberlain fought that day, as did Oates, with family nearby. His brother Tom was a lieutenant in Company G. His brother John was doing field-hospital work for the Christian Commission. As the armies were setting up earlier in the day, Chamberlain and his brothers were riding together when "a solid shot drawing close past our faces disturbed me. 'Boys,' I said, 'I don't like this. Another such shot might make it hard for mother.'" Chamberlain would also write that "as we neared the summit of the mountain, the shot so raked the crest that we had to keep our men below to save their heads, although this did not wholly avert the visits of tree-tops and splinters of rocks and iron."

Vincent's orders to Chamberlain had been clear: "'You understand. You are to hold this ground at all costs.' I did understand—full well; but had more to learn about costs."

The top of Little Round Top, photographed shortly after the battle. This is the point where the Union line turned to the left to protect against the Confederates' attempt to get in behind their position. Equipment discarded by soldiers is also visible.

Chamberlain and his men met charge after charge of Oates and his Alabamians. Chamberlain wrote: "The two lines met and broke and mingled in shock. The crush of musketry gave way to cuts and thrusts, grappling and wrestling. The edge of conflict swayed to and fro with wild whirlpools and eddies. At times I saw around me more of the enemy than my own men." As the fighting continued, one of Chamberlain's officers noticed something ominous—some of Oates's men were leaving the fighting line and moving to their right. It appeared that Oates was trying to outflank the 20th Maine.

Chamberlain decided to form his troops with a right angle on the left side of his line: "I immediately stretched my regiment to the left, by taking intervals to the left flank, and at the same time 'refusing' my left wing, so that it was nearly at right angles with my right." Chamberlain noted in his report that "this movement was executed under fire, the right wing keeping up fire, without giving the enemy any occasion to seize or even to suspect their advantage." They barely made it into position to stop Oates's attack, "but we were not a moment too soon; the enemy's flanking columns having gained their desired direction, burst upon my left, where they evidently had expected an unguarded flank." Chamberlain's report detailed charges and countercharges: "The edge of the fight rolled backward and forward like a wave. The dead and wounded were now in our front and then in our rear."

But all of Chamberlain's great tactics were not enough to stop the Confederates; because now his men, still under furious attack, were running out of ammunition: "My ammunition was soon exhausted. My men were firing their last shot and getting ready to 'club' their muskets. It was imperative to strike before we were struck by this overwhelming force in a

The same scene as in the preceding picture, photographed today. Note the same large rocks on the left side; they still look much the same as they did during the battle.

W. Michael Beller

hand-to-hand fight, which we could not probably have withstood or survived. At that crisis I ordered the bayonet."

Then Chamberlain gave the order that would not only earn him a promotion but would also earn him a place in history. With no ammunition, and under bitter attack, no one would have thought Chamberlain a coward to retreat, but he ordered a charge. In reserve on the left of the line, Company B joined in on their own initiative when they saw the opportunity and "fell upon the enemy as they were breaking, and by [Captain Morrill's] demonstrations, as well as his well-directed fire, added much to the effect of the charge."

For the Alabamians it was the last straw. Many men surrendered, and the rest retreated down the slope and partly up the side of Big Round Top. Joshua L. Chamberlain and his 20th Maine had held the Union line. It was an incredible feat, and much of the credit goes to Chamberlain himself, who saw the opportunities of his position and used them fully. Colonel Oates would write in his own memoirs about his enemy that day, "There never were harder fighters than the Twentieth Maine men and their gallant Colonel. His skill and persistence, and the great bravery of his men saved Little Round Top and the Army of the Potomac from defeat."

The rest of the Union line on Little Round Top had also held its ground. General Gouverneur Warren had come again to inspect the Union position on Little Round Top at the most critical moment. He found the Union line under terrible pressure. He ordered Brigadier General Stephen H. Weed's Brigade of fifteen hundred men, already on the march to support troops elsewhere, to attack the Confederates. The fresh Union troops sent the Confederates into a bloody retreat down the slope of Little Round Top.

CHAPTER 8

AFTER THE BATTLE
THE DEAD AND THE WOUNDED

Of the men from the 20th Maine who joined in battle that afternoon, many would never return. The Twentieth Maine Monument, placed at the far end of the left side of the line held by that unit on July 2, 1863, lists the names of the thirty-eight men killed in the fighting that day. Along with their names is the following message:

> HERE THE TWENTIETH MAINE REGIMENT COLONEL J. L. CHAMBERLAIN COMMANDING, FORMING THE EXTREME LEFT OF THE NATIONAL LINE OF BATTLE, ON THE 2ND DAY OF JULY, 1863 REPULSED THE ATTACK OF THE EXTREME RIGHT OF LONGSTREET'S CORPS AND CHARGED IN TURN, CAPTURING 308 PRISONERS. THE REGIMENT LOST 38 KILLED OR MORTALLY WOUNDED AND 93 WOUNDED OUT OF 358 ENGAGED. THIS MONUMENT ERECTED BY SURVIVORS OF THE REGIMENT AD 1886 MARKS VERY NEARLY THE SPOT WHERE THE COLORS STOOD.

For the men of the 15th Alabama, it was an even worse story. The 20th Maine had taken over three hundred prisoners, including twelve officers, from the four Confederate units on that hill. Only four hundred men of the five hundred in the 15th Alabama had been involved in the fight. Others had dropped out from the long, exhausting march or had been part of the canteen detail. But Colonel Oates wrote of their final stand, "My dead and wounded were then nearly as great in number as those still on duty. They literally covered the ground. The blood stood in puddles in some places on the rocks; the ground was soaked with the blood of as brave men as ever fell on the red field of battle." At battle's end, when the roll was called, only 223 answered. Oates reported officially, "17 killed, 54 wounded, and 90 missing, most of whom are either killed or wounded."

But it is in the individual stories that the horror of the fighting comes through. Private Gerrish wrote of his tent mate, Sergeant Charles Steele, "with a fatal wound" telling his captain "I am going, Captain" and dying "weltering in his blood." He remembered that Sergeant Lathrop, "with his brave heart and gigantic frame, fell dying with a frightful wound." He wrote of others "all severely wounded, and nearly all disabled."

Joshua Lawrence Chamberlain would remember the carnage and death as an "appalling sight." He described the scene as "a whole battery of shot and shell cutting a ragged chasm" through the lines. And he described "muskets dropped with death's quick relax, or clutched with last, convulsive energy, men falling like grass before the scythe." He watched one dying private, George Washington Buck of Company H, and promoted him to sergeant for his "noble courage on the field of Gettysburg."

Company F, of the 20th Maine, which carried the flag, lost all of its corporals and one sergeant. Company A had six corporals and two sergeants killed or wounded. One estimate says that probably twenty thousand bullets were fired at the 358

Three Confederate prisoners after the Battle of Gettysburg. Notice how poorly they are dressed and equipped. By this time in the Civil War, Confederate soldiers were sorely lacking in equipment and supplies.

men of the 20th Maine in that short few hours of battle on July 2. The report filed by the Maine Commissioners on the Maine units who fought during the battle included a description of a tree on the hill of Little Round Top: "One tree, some three or four inches through, in front of the left of company F, was cut entirely off about two feet above the ground. The ragged edges of the cut showed that it was made by bullets, and not by a shell." It is no wonder that so many soldiers were killed or wounded on that hill that afternoon.

Chamberlain himself had received two minor wounds during the battle, one when a piece of shell pierced his boot and cut his instep, the other when a minié ball bruised his thigh. Colonel Chamberlain was very fortunate that his thigh wound was fairly minor, since Civil War rifle bullets frequently caused severe injuries. His brother John, working at the field hospital, saw the men of the 20th Maine as they were brought from the field. As each new load of men arrived he looked fearfully to see if either of his two brothers was among them. But it had not been "a hard day for mother." Both brothers had only minor wounds.

Colonel Oates would not be so lucky. Lieutenant John A. Oates, the colonel's younger brother, lay on the field "pierced through by a number of bullets." Of his officers, Lieutenant Colonel Isaac B. Feagin "was shot through the knee" as he crossed Plum Run, and had to have his leg amputated. Several others were also killed or wounded. Captain Brainard, whom Oates described as "one of the bravest and best officers in the regiment," went down calling out, "Oh, God! that I could see my mother." Eighteen-year-old Lieutenant Cody "fell near my [Oates's] brother, mortally wounded."

This photograph, taken after the battle, looks south from Little Round Top toward the area known as the Slaughter Pen or the Valley of Death because of all the soldiers who were killed or wounded in this area. Big Round Top is in the background.

Oates watched Captain J. Henry Ellison die, wearing a "very fine captain's uniform which I had presented to him after my promotion." Writing forty years later, the horror of his friend's death was still clear: "I saw the ball strike him; that is, I was looking at him when it did. He fell upon his left shoulder, turned upon his back, raised his arms, clenched his fists, gave one shudder, his arms fell, and he was dead...the finest specimen of manhood that ever went down upon a field of carnage."

Of the common soldiers in his unit, Oates simply said, "the carnage in the ranks was appalling." He did tell of one soldier named Keils, of Company H, who "had his throat cut by a bullet, and he ran past me breathing at his throat and the blood spattering. His wind-pipe was entirely severed, but notwithstanding he crossed the mountain." Keils died the next morning.

Oates had tried to convince his younger brother not to fight that day, as he had been sick. John had replied, "Brother, I will not do it. If I were to remain here people would say that I did it through cowardice; no, sir . . . I shall go through unless I am killed." Oates recollected, "These were the last words ever passed between us." John was taken prisoner by the Union troops and died twenty-three days later in a Union hospital. Oates wrote of the care his brother and other Confederates received from a Dr. Reid, of the 155th Pennsylvania, who "did all that he could for them and had them decently buried when they died."

Oates wrote a lot about the pain and frustration of having to leave his wounded soldiers behind to be captured. He talked also of learning that some of his wounded were left on the field

Dead Confederate soldiers in the Slaughter Pen.

for two or three days before receiving medical care. He wrote of one soldier, Sergeant Johns, of Company B, who was shot in the thigh, and "lay where he fell in all the hard rain of the 3d and 4th days of July. . . . He lay on his back, could not turn, and kept from drowning by putting his hat over his face." Amazingly, he survived.

Oates wrote that "the wounded were removed to the Federal field hospital, where they were as well cared for as wounded soldiers in the hands of an enemy ever are." Eight of his soldiers' names and descriptions of their treatments can be found in the records of a Vermont surgeon, Henry Janes, who was in charge of the Union army hospitals after the battle. Of the eight, six eventually recovered and were discharged to City Point, Virginia, as prisoners waiting to be exchanged. The description of their care seems to indicate that they were treated as well as the Union soldiers whose records are on the same pages.

The deaths of two Alabamians left behind in the Union hospitals did not occur until late August. Private H. K. Norris, age twenty-two, died of gangrene on August 29, 1863, from a chest wound. By August 11, the records said he was failing rapidly, with pain and a severe cough. By August 25, the doctor reported "gangrene rapidly spreading, great difficulty of breathing." It was a lingering death.

From his medical records, John N. Sheppard looked to be recovering, until August 15, when the doctors noticed "pus burrowing above and below the wound." Eleven days later he was dead of pyemia, or blood poisoning. For those defeated Confederate soldiers, what a long, lonely time it must have been until the battle finally ended for them forever.

Dead Union soldiers were buried first. By the time the first photographers reached Gettysburg a few days after the battle, there were still some unburied Confederates left on the field.

Library of Congress

CHAPTER 9

AFTER THE BATTLE

FOR THE LIVING, THE WAR GOES ON

"Dear Fanny, We are fighting gloriously. Our loss is terrible but we are beating the Rebels as they were never beaten before. The 20th has immortalized itself. We had the post of honor in the severe fight of the 2d, on the extreme left where the enemy made a fierce attempt to turn the flank. . . . I am receiving all sorts of praise, but bear it meekly." In this letter to his wife, dated July 4, 1863, Joshua Lawrence Chamberlain already knew how famous their fight had become. He and his men would be receiving much praise to "bear . . . meekly" over the next several months of fighting.

The 20th Maine's day on July 2 did not end with the retreat of Oates and the Alabamians. At nine that night, the 20th Maine was ordered to move from its position and take a new position on the top of Big Round Top. The Union leaders wanted to finish the job they had started and protect the left end of the line completely. The 20th Maine (or rather, the two hundred exhausted men left of the 20th Maine) moved to their new positions with bayonets fixed, as they still had not been resupplied with ammunition.

Totally separated from the rest of the Union army, they held the Union line that evening, while under attack from

Confederate sharpshooters. Finally, later that night, they were joined by the 83rd Pennsylvania, who brought more ammunition with them. It was a tense ending to a long day. The Union men expected the Rebels to attack again at any moment and they knew that they could not possibly hold their position against a well-supported attack. But the attack never came, though the men were involved in several small skirmishes.

The next morning the 20th Maine was relieved and sent to the rear as reserve troops. There they sat out the major attack by the Confederate army on the center of the Union line. This attack, known as Pickett's Charge because it was led by Major General George E. Pickett, was the last major attempt by the Confederates to win the three-day battle.

On the morning of July 4, with the field cleared of the Confederate army, it was time to bury the dead where they had fallen on Little Round Top, "marking each grave by a headboard made of ammunition boxes with each dead soldier's name cut upon it." The bodies were later moved to the new Gettysburg National Cemetery. In his memoir, Private Gerrish would wish that "they had been left where they fell, on the rugged brow of Round Top, amid the battle-scarred rocks which they baptized with their blood." The Confederate dead were also buried, in one large common grave.

Oates and his 15th Alabama had only 223 enlisted men and 19 officers to answer roll call as they reassembled on the other side of Big Round Top on the evening of July 2. Others would straggle in during that night and early the next morning. The 15th Alabama held that position until ordered to withdraw about a half mile south in the late afternoon of July 3. They remained in that new location until evening, when they found

Field near Gettysburg
July 4th 1863.

Dear Fanny,

We are fighting
gloriously. Our loss is
terrible, but we are beating
the Rebels as they were never
beaten before.

The 20th has immortalized
itself. We had the post of
honor in the severe fight of
the 2d, on the extreme left
where the enemy made a
fierce attempt to turn the
flank. My Regt was the
extreme left. & was attacked
by a whole Brigade.
We not only held our ground
but charged on the Rebels
& drove them out of all sight

Library of Congress

Joshua Lawrence Chamberlain's letter home to his wife, Fanny, written in pencil on July 4, 1863, from a "Field near Gettysburg."

themselves totally isolated from the rest of the Confederate army. The messenger sent to order them to withdraw further had never reached them.

Now there were Union troops a short distance in front of them. So Oates ordered his men to retreat: "The Union army had advanced, and I was nearly surrounded, and happened to take the only safe retreat. Had I obeyed orders I and all of those with me would have finished our service as prisoners of war, a thing I always dreaded more than the bullets of the enemy." Eventually they located the rest of Longstreet's corps, and the Confederate army began its retreat on July 5.

Of course the war would continue. Although this would be the High-Water Mark of the Confederacy, the war would not end until April 1865. The 20th Maine followed the Confederate army into Virginia and spent the rest of 1863 involved in many skirmishes and minor battles there. In 1864 it would be involved in major battles at Spotsylvania Court House, near Chancellorsville, and at Petersburg, south of Richmond, Virginia.

On June 18, 1864, Colonel Chamberlain was badly wounded at Petersburg. Shot in the hip at a critical moment in the battle, he stood his ground, leaning on his sword. He was afraid his men might falter if they saw him fall. Finally he had no choice and slipped to the ground, still giving orders. Although he was bleeding badly, the fighting was heavy enough that he could not be removed from the field for well over an hour. When he reached the field hospital later that day, the doctors operated on him but did not expect him to survive. The next morning he wrote a good-bye letter to his wife.

Hearing of Chamberlain's gallant stand on the field and his

bravery in continuing his command after being wounded, General Ulysses S. Grant promoted him to brigadier general. To everyone's surprise, Chamberlain did recover and was able to accept command of the First Brigade on November 18, 1864, only five months after nearly dying.

The war also continued for the 15th Alabama. By the end of the four years, this regiment had seen action in forty-eight battles. Colonel Oates himself was seriously wounded at Chattanooga in November 1863: "I was shot through my right hip and thigh, the ball striking the thigh bone one inch below the hip joint, slightly fracturing it. . . . My boot was running over with blood, and the wound made it very painful for me to ride." Later in the war, on August 16, 1864, Oates lost his right arm in the fighting at Russell's Mills, near Petersburg. But even so, he was determined to return to command. In January 1865 he was offered some administrative duties, but he refused. He wanted to go back and fight, even though his shoulder, where the arm had been amputated, continued to "swell up again and pain me considerably." Confederate Secretary of War General Breckinridge offered Oates command of a brigade in General Johnston's army, but sent him home to recover first. The war ended before Oates could return to duty.

When the war finally ended, it was General Joshua Lawrence Chamberlain and the men he commanded (including what was left of the 20th Maine) who were given the honor of being in charge of the surrender of the Confederate Army of Northern Virginia. General Ulysses S. Grant, in command of all the Union armies, had negotiated the peace with General Robert E. Lee, in command of all the Confederate armies, on

Some dead Confederate soldiers partially buried on the battlefield. Many historians feel that they were buried by other Confederate soldiers before the retreat from the battlefield, because they have rough "headstones" to identify them. Most of the dead Confederates were unknown and could not be given marked graves.

April 9, 1865, at Appomattox Court House, Virginia. Now Grant ordered a dignified, simple ceremony in which the Confederate soldiers would pass in review and surrender their weapons and flags.

General Chamberlain conducted the "passing of the armies" on April 12, 1865. It would be hard for these proud Southern soldiers to march in review and turn in their flags and arms. They had fought hard for a cause they believed in. Chamberlain agreed with General Grant that they should not be humiliated as they admitted their defeat. The Union army under Chamberlain's command stood in respectful silence as the first of the Confederates passed by. A Union bugle sounded, and the Union army saluted the defeated Confederate army as it passed in review. Confederate General Gordon, leading the column, was touched by the gesture and ordered the Confederates to return the salute. It was a solemn, moving ceremony that allowed for honor on both sides. Both leaders that day would remember it. Gordon would call Chamberlain "one of the knightliest soldiers" in the Union for his gesture. Chamberlain would remember the Union troops standing with "not a cheer, nor word nor whisper of vain-glorying . . . but an awed stillness rather, and breath-holding, as if it were the passing of the dead."

Field hospital of the Union Second Corps after the battle. Many of the soldiers, especially earlier in the war, were cared for in much dirtier and less well maintained field hospitals.

CHAPTER 10

AFTER THE WAR

GOVERNOR OATES OF ALABAMA

William Calvin Oates would remain bitter about his afternoon on Little Round Top for the rest of his life. "No battle in the world's history ever had greater consequences dependent upon it," he wrote in 1905, "nor so many mishaps, or lost opportunities—especially on the side of the Confederates—as that of Gettysburg." His only praise was for Confederate commander Robert E. Lee: "Lee's strategy was superb, but the execution of his plans was bungling." He detailed every mistake made by the Confederates that day, including the decision not to allow him to take a position on Great Round Top, as he called it, which would "have enabled the Confederates to win the field." Throughout his book he listed all the mistakes made by the Confederate government and military leaders during the war. At the very end he called the Confederate government "incompetent" and blamed it for losing the war.

When he wrote his memoirs there was another issue that Oates was very angry about. This was the claim that the North had won the war because God was on its side and not on the side of the slaveholding South. He wrote, "I would never go to war unless I conscientiously believed that the cause was just. . . . When we went to war it was a matter of business, of difference among men about their temporal affairs. God had nothing to do with it."

In some ways this was the same "fighting Oates" from before the war. In the time between the end of the war and when he wrote his memoirs Oates led a full life. The part of him that carried over from his youth was his love of a good fight. But now this was directed and disciplined. He fought well on the political battlefields after the war.

Oates had lost his arm, but that would not hinder him from going back to practicing law in Alabama when the Civil War ended in 1865. After the excitement of the Civil War, practicing law in Abbeville was not enough for him. He first was elected to the Alabama legislature in 1870 and then to the United States House of Representatives. He was reelected seven times and only resigned when he was elected governor of Alabama in 1894. Oates only served one term as governor, but he is remembered for his financial ability and his improvements in the prison system. He ran for the United States Senate in 1897 but lost.

During all those years of public service he became famous as "the advocate of good laws, regardless of their political origin." It is amazing how often the actions of his political career were described in military terms, such as *combated, fought, opposed,* and *pressed.*

Then he was given the opportunity to become a soldier again when the Spanish-American War broke out in 1898. President William McKinley appointed him a brigadier general in the United States Army, and he commanded the U.S. Volunteers.

William Calvin Oates in 1900.

For many old Civil War veterans this war was a chance to relive their youthful past. Many who wanted commissions, including Oates's old adversary Joshua Lawrence Chamberlain, could not get them. For Oates it was a fitting end to his long career of government service. He had begun with military service to the Confederacy, served both Alabama and the United States well as a politician, and now would end with military service to the United States.

Along the way, on March 28, 1882, at age forty-seven, Oates finally married. He and his wife, Sallie Toney, from Eufald, Alabama, had one child, William Calvin Jr.

Oates did not live as long as his old enemy, Joshua Lawrence Chamberlain, but died September 9, 1910, in Montgomery, Alabama, at the age of seventy-four.

CHAPTER 11

AFTER THE WAR

GOVERNOR CHAMBERLAIN OF MAINE

The wounded Joshua Lawrence Chamberlain returned home to Maine a hero in August 1865. Everyone rushed to honor him.

Chamberlain resumed his position as professor of rhetoric and oratory at Bowdoin College, but his injuries bothered him so much that he could not keep up with his teaching schedule. More surgery was needed. Chamberlain was also restless and found it hard to go back to being a college professor after his exciting military career. Fortunately, he was not to be one for long.

The Republican party leaders of Maine invited Chamberlain to run for governor, and, in September 1866, he won the position by the largest majority ever in Maine's history. He was a strong, activist governor, who made his voice heard on national issues as well as on state issues. He was reelected to three more one-year terms after his first one and was governor until 1870.

While governor, Chamberlain was awarded an honorary doctorate by Bowdoin College, and after his term of office was finished, it was no surprise when Bowdoin selected him as its next president. So again Bowdoin became his home. First as a student, then as a professor, and finally as president Joshua Lawrence Chamberlain was involved with Bowdoin for over sixty-five years.

From his home in Brunswick he would continue his involvement in worldwide events. In 1878 he took his long-delayed trip to Europe to attend the Paris Universal Exposition as an official representative of United States education. In 1880 he tried for election as a United States senator but, like his old enemy William Oates, he was unsuccessful. Both men were governors. Both men wanted to be senators. Neither would win that prize.

In 1883 Chamberlain resigned his presidency at Bowdoin. It was time for him to undergo more surgery for his old wounds. He would return to teach at the college occasionally, and he remained a member of the college's board of trustees until his death, but his official tenure was over. Other colleges tried to hire him, but he refused their offers.

Chamberlain remained active in Civil War veterans' organizations. He headed Maine's Grand Army of the Republic and its Military Order of the Loyal Legion. He visited the scenes of his important battles many times, and on October 3, 1888, when the monuments to Maine soldiers at Gettysburg were dedicated, Chamberlain was named "president of the day" and gave a speech that everyone praised.

Chamberlain, the teacher of rhetoric and oratory, knew how to give a long oration with great moral themes. In his speech he reminded all the Maine soldiers that "we fought no better, perhaps, than they [the soldiers of the 15th Alabama]. We exhibited, perhaps, no higher individual qualities. But the cause for which we fought was higher; our thought was wider." He

Joshua Lawrence Chamberlain in 1905.

praised his listeners for their deeds, then warned them not to be too proud: "Grave responsibilities come with great victory. The danger is not . . . from renewed attacks of those who lost, as from the tendencies of power on the part of those who won." Chamberlain also managed to capture the sacredness of the battlefield: "In great deeds something abides. On great fields something stays. Forms change and pass; bodies disappear; but spirits linger; to consecrate ground for the vision-place of souls."

Chamberlain the orator, Chamberlain the statesman, Chamberlain the political leader—whatever the role, he filled it with honor and dignity in the years after 1865. There was one more role he sought, however, that he did not gain. His old adversary, William Oates, served as a brigadier general in the Spanish-American War. Chamberlain offered his services, but they were not accepted. He was almost seventy years old and still suffered from his Civil War wounds, and there were many younger, healthier retired officers to choose from.

Chamberlain outlived his wife, Fanny, who died in 1905. He remained close to his two children, Grace and Harold Wyllys, and to his grandchildren. As the years passed, his old wounds bothered him more and more, and finally on February 24, 1914, Chamberlain died at the age of eighty-five. He had two funeral services. The first was a military funeral in Portland. The second was at the church at Bowdoin College with speeches by Bowdoin faculty and alumni.

CHAPTER 12
THE FINAL SCENE

Today at Gettysburg simple monuments mark the place of the bitter fighting of that hot July afternoon in 1863. In time the battle for Little Round Top was overshadowed by Pickett's Charge, which took place the following day. Gettysburg itself has never been forgotten, both as the High-Water Mark of the Confederacy and as the site of Abraham Lincoln's dedication in November 1863.

Over the years the decisions of July 2 have been debated back and forth. Oates was not the only one to be bitter about Confederate military leadership that day. Chamberlain was not the only one to see final victory going to the side that was "right." The Civil War continued to be fought in words by the men who had fought it in deeds.

Oates claimed that General Lee was looking for a victory at Gettysburg as a key to winning the entire war and wrote, "Had he won that battle, his objective point was Philadelphia, Pennsylvania, and he could not have been checked. Washington and Baltimore would have fallen, and thousands of prisoners who would have been released from Fort McHenry, Point Lookout and other prisons, and the volunteers from Maryland who would have joined Lee, would have made him resistless, and negotiations for peace would have followed."

Whatever might have happened, Oates and his Alabamians could not defeat Chamberlain and his 20th Maine on Little Round Top on July 2. And the Confederate army was driven from Pennsylvania in defeat after the three-day battle.

Both sides knew, however, that the end of the Civil War began there. The 20th Maine's Private Gerrish said it best: "The Confederacy had received its death blow. New armies could be raised, munitions of war purchased, campaigns planned, and scores of bloody battles fought but all this was to be but the heroism of despair. The prestige lost in the Pennsylvania campaign could not be regained. The fate of the Confederacy was but a question of time."

President Abraham Lincoln came to Gettysburg in November 1863 to dedicate a national cemetery there for burial of the soldiers who had died in the battle. In one of the most famous speeches in all of American history, he spoke about the battlefield and the people who had fought and died there. As President Lincoln stated in his Gettysburg Address, "In a larger sense, we cannot dedicate—we cannot consecrate—we cannot hallow this ground. The brave men, living and dead, who struggled here, have consecrated it, far above our poor power to add or detract."

Joshua Lawrence Chamberlain saw the battleground where the 20th Maine and the 15th Alabama fought the same way Lincoln did. He wrote, "No chemistry of frost or rain, no overlapping mould of the season's recurrent life and death, can ever separate from the soil of these consecrated fields the life-blood so deeply commingled and incorporate here." The 20th Maine had held "this ground at all costs," as Colonel Vincent had ordered. But the blood of both the 20th Maine and 15th

Alabama had consecrated that ground together. Enemies on July 2, 1863, on a little hill in Gettysburg, Pennsylvania, the survivors of these two brave regiments would be united as fellow countrymen again when the Civil War came to an end.

Sources for Research

Brake, Robert L. Collection. U.S. Army Military History
  Institute, Carlisle, Pennsylvania.
Chamberlain, Joshua Lawrence. Papers, 1862–1910.
  Manuscript Division, Library of Congress, Washington, D.C.
Frassanito, William A. *Gettysburg: A Journey in Time.* New York:
  Charles Scribner's Sons, 1975.
Gerrish, Theodore. *Army Life: A Private's Reminiscences of the
  Civil War.* Portland, Maine: Hoyt, Fogg & Donham, 1882.
Janes, Henry. *Notes of some of the gunshot injuries . . .* Special
  Collections. Bailey/Howe Library, University of Vermont,
  Burlington, Vermont.
Krick, Robert K. *Lee's Colonels.* Dayton, Ohio: Morningside, 1979.
Maine at Gettysburg. Portland, Maine: Maine Gettysburg
  Commission, 1898.
Nofi, Albert A. *The Gettysburg Campaign.* New York:
  Gallery Books, 1986.
Norton, Oliver Wilcox. *The Attack and Defense of Little Round Top.*
  New York: Neale Publishing Company, 1913.
Oates, William C. *The War Between the Union and the Confederacy.*
  New York: Neale Publishing Company, 1905.
Owen, Thomas McAdory. *History of Alabama and Dictionary of
  Alabama Biography.* Reprint edition. Spartanburg, South
  Carolina: The Reprint Company, 1978.

Pfanz, Harry W. *Gettysburg: The Second Day.* Chapel Hill:
University of North Carolina Press, 1987.

Pullen, John J. *The Twentieth Maine.* Philadelphia:
J. B. Lippincott, 1957.

Trulock, Alice Rains. *In the Hands of Providence.* Chapel Hill:
University of North Carolina Press, 1992.

*War of the Rebellion: A Compilation of the Official Records of the
Union and Confederate Armies.* Washington, D.C.:
Government Printing Office, 1889.

Wheeler, Richard. *Witness to Gettysburg.* New York:
Harper & Row, 1987.

Whitman, William E. S., and Charles H. True. *Maine in the War
for the Union.* Lewiston, Maine: Nelson Dingley Jr. & Co.,
1865.

INDEX

W

Warren, Gouverneur, 42, *43*,
53–54, 60
Washington, D.C., 21, 86
water, lack of, 44, 46
weapons, *16*, 29
Weed's Brigade, 60

winter, 15, 37–38
wounded soldiers, 30
Chamberlain as, 73, 74, 82,
83, 85
from Little Round Top, 62,
64, 66, 68
Oates as, 74